For Frances, who builds books
S. S.

For Time Out in Mount Eden
B. L.

Text copyright © 2014 by Sally Sutton
Illustrations copyright © 2014 by Brian Lovelock

First U.S. edition 2014

Library of Congress Catalog Card Number 2013953459
ISBN 978-0-7636-7325-3

CCP 19
10 9 8 7 6 5 4

Printed in Shenzhen, Guangdong, China

This book was typeset in Franklin Gothic Extra Bold Condensed.
The illustrations were done in pigmented inks.

Candlewick Press
99 Dover Street
Somerville, Massachusetts 02144

visit us at www.candlewick.com

CONSTRUCTION

SALLY SUTTON · ILLUSTRATED BY BRIAN LOVELOCK

CANDLEWICK PRESS

Dig the ground. Dig the ground.

Bore down in the mud.

Shove the piles in one by one.

Fill the holes. Fill the holes.

Let the concrete drop.

Spread it fast before it sets.

Hoist the wood. Hoist the wood.

Chain and hook and strap.

Swing it round, then lower it down.

Cut the planks. Cut the planks.
Measure, mark, and saw.
Earmuffs will protect your ears.

Wizz!

ZIZZ!

ROAR!

Build the frame. Build the frame.

Hammer all day long.

Make the stairs and floors and walls.

Raise the roof. Raise the roof.

Drive the screws in now.

Power tools will do the job.

Ring!
ZING!
POW!

Build the sides. Build the sides.
Fit the doors in too.
Lift the windows
into place.

Lay the pipes. Lay the pipes.

Twist and turn and click.

Run the wires so you'll have power.

Scritch!

SWITCH!

FLICK!

Spread the paint. Spread the paint.

Bend and stretch and stoop.

Let it dry, then paint some more.

Glug!
GLOP!
GLOOP!

Fill the rooms. Fill the rooms.

Join the hustle-bustle.

Chairs and tables, shelves and books.

Scrape! THUMP! RUSTLE!

Choose your books. Choose your books.

Borrow all you need.

The library's here for everyone.

Ready... STEADY... READ!

MACHINE FACTS

LOADER CRANE: A loader crane has an articulated arm that fits onto a truck and is used to load and unload heavy things.

MOBILE CRANE: A truck-mounted crane that can lift heavy materials from one place and move them to another. Its arm can move up and down and swing from side to side.

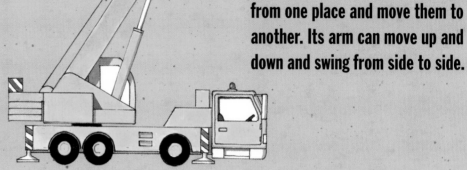

EXCAVATOR: Excavators dig the ground. This excavator has an auger attachment. It drills holes for the building's foundation piles.

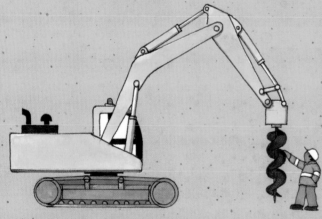

CONSTRUCTION WORKER:

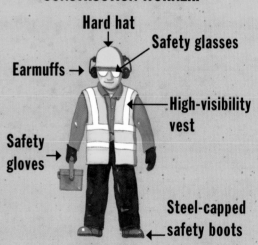

Hard hat

Safety glasses

Earmuffs →

← High-visibility vest

Safety gloves

Steel-capped safety boots

CONCRETE PUMPING TRUCK: A pumping truck has a long arm called a boom. Wet concrete is pumped through a hose in the boom to any part of the construction site.

Builders on a big construction site need lots of special clothing and equipment to stay safe.

CONCRETE MIXING TRUCK: This truck mixes cement, sand, and gravel to make liquid concrete. It feeds the concrete into a pumping truck.